The Good Counselor

by Kathryn Grant

A Samuel French Acting Edition

New York Hollywood London Toronto

SAMUELFRENCH.COM

Copyright © 2007, 2008, 2011 by Kathryn Grant
ALL RIGHTS RESERVED

CAUTION: Professionals and amateurs are hereby warned that *THE GOOD COUNSELOR* is subject to a Licensing Fee. It is fully protected under the copyright laws of the United States of America, the British Commonwealth, including Canada, and all other countries of the Copyright Union. All rights, including professional, amateur, motion picture, recitation, lecturing, public reading, radio broadcasting, television and the rights of translation into foreign languages are strictly reserved. In its present form the play is dedicated to the reading public only.

The amateur and professional live stage performance rights to *THE GOOD COUNSELOR* are controlled exclusively by Samuel French, Inc., and licensing arrangements and performance licenses must be secured well in advance of presentation. PLEASE NOTE that amateur Licensing Fees are set upon application in accordance with your producing circumstances. When applying for a licensing quotation and a performance license please give us the number of performances intended, dates of production, your seating capacity and admission fee. Licensing Fees are payable one week before the opening performance of the play to Samuel French, Inc., at 45 W. 25th Street, New York, NY 10010.

Licensing Fee of the required amount must be paid whether the play is presented for charity or gain and whether or not admission is charged.

Professional/stock licensing fees quoted upon application to Samuel French, Inc.

For all other rights than those stipulated above, apply to: Bret Adams, Ltd., 448 West 44th Street, New York, NY 10036; attn: Alexis Williams.

Particular emphasis is laid on the question of amateur or professional readings, permission and terms for which must be secured in writing from Samuel French, Inc.

Copying from this book in whole or in part is strictly forbidden by law, and the right of performance is not transferable.

Whenever the play is produced the following notice must appear on all programs, printing and advertising for the play: "Produced by special arrangement with Samuel French, Inc."

Due authorship credit must be given on all programs, printing and advertising for the play.

ISBN 978-0-573-69912-2   Printed in U.S.A.   #29804

No one shall commit or authorize any act or omission by which the copyright of, or the right to copyright, this play may be impaired.

No one shall make any changes in this play for the purpose of production.

Publication of this play does not imply availability for performance. Both amateurs and professionals considering a production are strongly advised in their own interests to apply to Samuel French, Inc., for written permission before starting rehearsals, advertising, or booking a theatre.

No part of this book may be reproduced, stored in a retrieval system, or transmitted in any form, by any means, now known or yet to be invented, including mechanical, electronic, photocopying, recording, videotaping, or otherwise, without the prior written permission of the publisher.

MUSIC USE NOTE

Licensees are solely responsible for obtaining formal written permission from copyright owners to use copyrighted music in the performance of this play and are strongly cautioned to do so. If no such permission is obtained by the licensee, then the licensee must use only original music that the licensee owns and controls. Licensees are solely responsible and liable for all music clearances and shall indemnify the copyright owners of the play and their licensing agent, Samuel French, Inc., against any costs, expenses, losses and liabilities arising from the use of music by licensees.

IMPORTANT BILLING AND CREDIT REQUIREMENTS

All producers of *THE GOOD COUNSELOR must* give credit to the Author of the Play in all programs distributed in connection with performances of the Play, and in all instances in which the title of the Play appears for the purposes of advertising, publicizing or otherwise exploiting the Play and/or a production. The name of the Author *must* appear on a separate line on which no other name appears, immediately following the title and *must* appear in size of type not less than fifty percent of the size of the title type.

Until August 1, 2013 producers in the United States and Canada must include in programs the following statement:

**Originally produced by Premiere Stages at
Kean University, Union, NJ.**

THE GOOD COUNSELOR was originally produced at Premiere Stages at Kean University in Union, New Jersey on July 15, 2010. The performance was directed by John Wooten, with sets by Joseph Gourley, lighting by Nadine Charlson, costumes by Karen Hart, sound by Charles Lawlor, and dramaturgy by Erica Nagel. The production stage manager was Dale Smallwood. The cast was as follows:

VINCENT.....................................Edward O'Blenis
RAY.. Erik LaRay Harvey
RITA.. Geany Masai
EVELYN................................Susan Louise O'Connor
MAIA .... Socorro Santiago

THE GOOD COUNSELOR was the winner of the 2010 Premiere Stages Play Festival and the 2010 Jerry Kaufman Award in Playwriting.

THE GOOD COUNSELOR, originally conceived as a creative dissertation under the title, *The Family Way*, was written in satisfaction of a Doctor of Letters degree from the Arts and Letters Program at Drew University in New Jersey under the guidance of Rosemary McLaughlin and Carol Wipf. Retitled *Wonderful Counselor* in 2006, it received further developmental support from the American Renaissance Theater Company, The Actors Studio Playwright and Director's Unit, the Ensemble Studio Theater, LAByrinth Theater Company, the Abingdon Theater, and the Barrow Group Theater. I am deeply grateful to all of the organizations and artists who participated in the development of this play.

–*KG*

CHARACTERS

VINCENT HEFFERNON (27-34 years old) is an African-American public defender practicing law in a rural county. He is the youngest in a family of four children and the only one in the family who has made it into the professional class. Vincent is sharp, mercurial and slick in some ways, altering his persona to suit the situation, but in other ways, he is fragile. He is not at ease with himself or reconciled to his position as the favored son in a struggling family.

RAY HEFFERNON (29-36 years old) is Vincent's older brother, an African-American man currently working as a roofer. He has a history of drug addiction that may mask an underlying mood disorder like bipolar.

RITA HEFFERNON (60-75 years old) is Ray and Vincent's mother. She is in poor health but struggles to stay out of bed and keep up appearances. Widowed at a young age, she raised her children on her own, takes pride in her autonomy and has little truck for those who aren't able to manage life's challenges. She has pushed some dark episodes in her life into a corner and finds refuge in her church and the teachings of the Bible.

EVELYN LAVERTY (20-30 years old) ia a single white mother currently a suspect in the death of her infant. Although she loves her remaining five-year old daughter, she had mixed feelings about her infant and insecurities about her competence as a mother. Before her incarceration, she drank to take the edge off of all the chaos that was piling up in her world. She is not an appealing candidate to put on the stand in court because she is scared, truculent and a knee-jerk racist.

MAYA ARUNA (45-70 years old) is the supervisor in the county's Office of the Public Defender. Originally the role was written for an Indian-American, but the role can be cast as a nationalized citizen born in South or Central America, Mexico, the Caribbean, one of the countries of the former Soviet Union, a South East Asian Country or any other country (not African) with large segments of the population living in poverty (change name as needed.) She has lived a good portion of her life in close proximity to the poor and she doesn't romanticize their lives. Her immigrant status gives her an outsider's perspective. She isn't mired in American views of motherhood and the management of families. Notwithstanding these differences, she is deeply patriotic and fervent about the possibilities of American jurisprudence. Both pragmatic and hopelessly liberal, she is what is known as a "public defense lifer," passionate about defending the poor, whether they are guilty of a crime or not.

AUTHOR'S NOTE

There are a number of stylistic challenges in the play, chiefly those that require the audience to accept leaps through time and place. I have included some ways that a production might resolve them, for example in John Wooten's production at Premiere Stages, when time shifted in the first act, the actor playing Vincent put a private school emblem on his blazer indicating that he was now a young man (thank you, John.) But there may be other ways to resolve these leaps using projections, sounds, lighting or music. I leave most of the details to the artists who will come up with innovations that will be right for their particulars of space, staff, available resources and audience.

For Ed.

ACT I

Prologue

(Two pools of light pick out **VINCENT** *and* **RITA** *on opposite sides of the stage.* **VINCENT**, *a public defender, delivers his closing argument in court. As he does this,* **RITA**, *prepares for church, humming a hymn.* **RITA** *is a woman in her 60s but she looks much older. Her body is riddled with arthritis and other middling afflictions. She is seated, wearing a slip, and putting cream on her body. When she is done, she sits back and catches her breath. She grabs onto a cane for support, she rocks back and forth a few times to find momentum, and then makes the push to stand. She finds her balance and stands still for a moment. In a way, she is magnificent. Finally sure, she then begins to put on her dress and shoes. As she performs these actions,* **VINCENT** *speaks.)*

VINCENT. A woman lives in our minds. She is clean, skin supple, hair fragrant and with soft arms open, she welcomes you into a pillowy embrace. She leads you through rooms that are quiet and cool, free of the day to day of dust and fingerprints. You come to a table heavy with your favorite foods, hot, steaming, succulent and with a voice, low and tuneful, she invites you to take your fill. And as you do, you become whole again. For to be in these rooms under the glow of her presence is never to want – she anticipates your every desire. And yet she seems to be without desire. She is contentment itself…so happy is she to be at your beck and call.

(pause)

VINCENT. In short, she is perfection just around the bend and a footstep out of reach. And she taunts you with the notion of the person you might have been had you been blessed with a mother such as she.

(pause)

This is the woman who is in our minds when we ask ourselves the question, "Is Evelyn Laverty a good mother?" I want you to put that woman aside for the moment. Don't worry, she won't go away. She is eternal.

*(Lights come down on **RITA** as **VINCENT** strides out of the courtroom and moves into another time and place.)*

Scene One

*(As **VINCENT** moves away from the courtroom lights come up on the living room of Rita Heffernon's house in a rural county two to three hours from a metropolitan center. It is a house that was built in the twenties to house factory workers. It can be depicted simply. Just some seating and a display shelf with portraits of young people graduating high school and an array of trophies and framed awards. **VINCENT** stands regarding his older brother, **RAY** who is eating some sweet rolls with sugar icing.)*

VINCENT. Mom make you those sweet rolls?

RAY. Yeah.

(pause)

Don't look at me like that.

VINCENT. She never makes them for me anymore.

RAY. Guess you're not the favorite.

VINCENT. Give me one of them bad boys.

*(He grabs at **RAY**'s plate and **RAY** gets up to get away from him.)*

RAY. Don't get all grabby and shit. I'll give you one.

(**VINCENT** *grabs his whole plate and walks away.*)

RAY. *(cont.)* Look at you. No better than a bread line skunk freak.

VINCENT. Shut up.

RAY. You got a bad case of the munchies. You bake when you wake?

VINCENT. *(laughing)* Oh, no, I leave the baking to you.

RAY. You're getting crumbs all over your suit.

VINCENT. *(Looking down.)* Shit!

RAY. Come here.

(Takes out a handkerchief and brushes Vincent off.)

Look at you. You can't go to church looking like that. You gonna' be a sanctified deacon, son.

VINCENT. Yeah, right.

(finishing off the roll)

I ate your roll. It was good.

RAY. There's more in the kitchen. You think I let you eat my last sweet roll!

(**VINCENT** *goes out to the kitchen, gets another couple of sweet rolls, gives one to* **RAY** *and sits down.*)

VINCENT. Mama told me about you doing the work down Crisfield.

RAY. Yeah.

VINCENT. Morton hook you up?

RAY. *(nodding)* He told me you called. Only guy who would see me.

VINCENT. He needed people.

RAY. No doubt. It's hot on them roofs.

VINCENT. Well, I think it's great you're working.

RAY. Yeah. It's great. Yeah. You try to get that tar and shit out your hair.

(He bends down to show his brother his head.)

Man I got a bald spot where that shit took me down to the scalp.

VINCENT. Ooooo, I can see that. Man! That is some raw shit.

RAY. You know that I am the only American on that roof. Bunch of Mexicans. They're teaching me Spanish. "Mucho trabaho, poco dinero."

VINCENT. That's good, man.

RAY. *(There is an awkward pause. He walks over to a hallway and calls.)* Hey woman, your other son is here.

RITA. *(shouting from offstage)* You boys aren't eating in my living room, getting crumbs on my clean covers are you?

RAY. *(calling in the same direction)* No, we ain't eating nothing.

(We hear the voice of **RITA** *singing "Blessed Assurance."* **RAY** *walks back toward* **VINCENT**.*)*

She's putting on her Sunday wig.

VINCENT. How do you know?

RAY. She's singing "Blessed Assurance."

VINCENT. You are one warped individual. You coming to church?

RAY. I don't know, man. Reverend Staunton'll try to save me. Get his quota for the month. Give me the whole deal. Total immersion, son. No doubt.

VINCENT. Oh, yeah!

RAY. He gets me in the baptismal pool, it'll be all over, you understand. He'll be keeping me under till I am seeing my whole life flashing –

VINCENT. And that ain't pretty!

RAY. Shit, that's butt ugly! But Mama, she's gonna walk into heaven on that day I get soaked.

VINCENT. *(getting into his groove)* She gonna walk on in all right!

RAY. What with her prodigal son swimmin' in the blood!

VINCENT. Oh, Lord!

RAY. *(getting into the spirit)* And then when she gets the spirit, it's gonna spread through that Church like swine flu! And then they all gonna' start going down!

VINCENT. Oh, they'll go down all right! You need some damn stretchers when that spirit starts working.

RAY. You'll need a regular fleet, son. Them ushers runnin' up and down the aisles draggin' them ladies out to the recovery room till it look like a Mash Unit. Perverted suckers lookin' up Mama's dress and all her garters poppin'!

VINCENT. *(laughing)* Stop buggin' on me, Ray.

RAY. *(laughter subsiding)* Gawd, she's a sight for sore eyes, when she gets the spirit!

VINCENT. That she is!

RAY. It's almost worth going to Church just to see her get juiced.

VINCENT. *(Pause. He stops laughing.)* Really?

RAY. That's what's left of Miss Rita, man.

VINCENT. Oh, come on. She's all right.

RITA. *(yelling from offstage)* What you boys doing in there?

VINCENT. Nothing!

RITA. Am I hearing cussin'?

RAY. *(calling)* Don't put that on me, lady. That's your baptized son talking now.

VINCENT. Thanks.

RAY. *(shouting off)* Get yourself together, woman. Time ain't waitin' on no one.

VINCENT. You just got here?

RAY. No, man. Come last night to mow the lawn. You're letting it slip.

VINCENT. Yeah. I been busy at work.

RAY. You're in the papers.

*(**RAY** picks up a paper laying on the coffee table. He gives it to **VINCENT**.)*

VINCENT. Damn, how this get out? Mama see it?

RAY. Oh, yeah. She ain't none happy about it either.

VINCENT. Well, I don't get to pick my clients.

RAY. She guilty? She kill the baby?

VINCENT. I don't know, man.

RAY. That's what you always say.

VINCENT. I suppose.

RAY. That's pretty cold…leaving a baby in a bean field.

VINCENT. Yeah.

RAY. Behind that section eight trailer park!

VINCENT. Yeah, right under the railroad trestle.

RAY. Crackerjack bullshit all over that piece of land.

VINCENT. Yeah, yeah. I saw that.

RAY. She a crackhead? Methmonster?

VINCENT. I don't know, man. I can't talk. You know that.

(changing the subject)

Where you stayin'?

RAY. With Naomi. I'm watching the kids on Saturday when she has to work weekends.

VINCENT. That's good. Ray?

RAY. You better get Mama outta' here. You'll never get a parking spot near the entrance. And you know how 46 gets all balled up with the church traffic.

VINCENT. It's good to see you like this.

RAY. Good to see you, too. You could go out 42 North… take the bypass…but there's a a lot of construction…

VINCENT. No, I mean…you know what I mean.

RAY. You mean, when I'm not fucked up.

VINCENT. Yeah. Kind of. Yeah.

RAY. Thanks!

VINCENT. Oh, come on.

RAY. It's kind of dry out there, man. Rooftop minimum wage shit!

VINCENT. Can I help with anything?

RAY. No, man, I'm cool.

VINCENT. I can hook you up with a doctor, with therapists, anything.
RAY. I told you, I'm cool.

(**VINCENT** *struggles with how to say this.*)

VINCENT. Can I say I know you don't want to hear –
RAY. Wait. Stop!
VINCENT. What?
RAY. Just stop!
VINCENT. No. No, man, I wouldn't say – I just wanted –
RAY. No, man. Uh-uh. Just don't say anything. You want to jinx me? You piece of preppy shit!

(**RAY** *reaches over and hits* **VINCENT** *on the back of the head.*)

VINCENT. Hey, what the –

(**VINCENT** *reaches up to fend off* **RAY** *who is swatting at him still.*)

RAY. *(as he continues the onslaught)* You did that last time I tried to dry out. No. Shut the hell up, you little punk.
VINCENT. Okay! Okay! Leave me alone! Watch it now, Mama gonna' –
RAY. I'll kick your ass, you try to school me!
VINCENT. Okay!

(*He hears footsteps.*)

Shhhhhh!
RAY. Good.

(**RITA** *walks in. She stands there with her gloves and purse, looking at the mess of crumbs on her slipcovers.*)

RITA. Would you look at the mess you made on my covers. What kind of grown men have I raised?

(**VINCENT** *takes out a handkerchief and sweeps the crumbs onto a plate.* **RITA** *looks at* **RAY.***)

Raymond, you didn't bring something better to wear?
RAY. Change my mind.

RITA. What?

RAY. I don't want to go to church, Mom.

RITA. *(after a pause, steeling herself for a fight)* Fine. But you are not staying in the house.

RAY. So what am I supposed –

VINCENT. Come on, Mom. Ray is fine.

RITA. You will not stay alone in my house. Uh-uh. No, sir. This house is going to be locked up. And you won't be in it. I don't care what you do. You can walk to the strip mall. Something is opened.

(reaches into her purse)

Here's five dollars.

RAY. I don't want your money.

VINCENT. We can drop him off at Naomi's –

RITA. We don't have time. Now come on, let's go. Check the stove, Vincent.

VINCENT. It's off.

RITA. You sure?

VINCENT. It's off.

RITA. All right then.

(pulling on her gloves)

Let's lock up the house. Get the back door.

VINCENT. Jesus Christ, Mama!

RAY. It's okay, Vin.

VINCENT. Is this really necessary?

RITA. *(grimly)* Yes. I would say so. Uh-huh.

RAY. *(looking at his mother)* Lock the door. Go on, man, lock it.

*(**VINCENT**, **RITA**, and **RAY** face off against each other.)*

Scene Two

*(Lights come down on the living room as **VINCENT** moves into a new area of the stage that suggests the interview room in a women's detention facility. We hear a clang as an unseen guard locks the door to an interview room. The sound echoes in a surreal way as it bounces off the concrete walls. **VINCENT** sits at a table with **EVELYN LAVERTY**, a white, 24 year-old, prisoner. **EVELYN** wears an orange jumpsuit. The sleeves are rolled up and you can see a large tattoo on her arm. The tattoo features a heart with the word "Pook" inscribed within it. Her sneakers don't have laces because she is on a "suicide watch." She has pulled out most of her eyelashes and eyebrows. **VINCENT** is clearly uncomfortable, trying to find his footing.)*

VINCENT. Okay. We're not going anywhere, Evelyn. We might as well talk to each other. Why don't you tell me what happened.

EVELYN. Can you get me some cough drops? It's dusty in here.

VINCENT. You can't just bring stuff in like that. It's got to be cleared. I'll do it tomorrow.

EVELYN. Smith Brothers, cherry.

VINCENT. Sure. No problem.

(silence)

EVELYN. Can you get me some lashes?

VINCENT. Sorry?

EVELYN. *(She is pulling at her raw lids.)* False eyelashes.

VINCENT. Maybe you stop doing that, you won't need false eyelashes.

EVELYN. It's a habit.

(She stops.)

VINCENT. How are you eating?

EVELYN. All right.

VINCENT. Sleeping okay?

EVELYN. I sleep.

VINCENT. *(looking at her tattoo)* Nice tattoo. Who's "Pook"?

EVELYN. None of your business.

VINCENT. Okay. So maybe it's time that we should talk about the baby…your son…David's death.

(pause)

EVELYN. You have to do this job don't you?

VINCENT. I take the clients they assign me.

EVELYN. You have to do it.

VINCENT. Well, actually, I choose to be here. I don't have to do this work.

EVELYN. So why do you do it?

VINCENT. I get paid to argue. I like that.

EVELYN. So get me –

VINCENT. *(sharply)* But I am not a whipping boy.

EVELYN. Look like one.

VINCENT. I look like a whipping boy and you look like someone in deep shit.

EVELYN. Fuck you, white bread.

VINCENT. Oh, I'm white?

EVELYN. You don't act black.

VINCENT. *(smiling)* And yet, people still treat me like I'm black.

*(**EVELYN** glares at him.)*

Evelyn. Ms. Laverty.

(During this speech he packs his note pad into a briefcase and puts on an overcoat.)

You may not like black folks telling you what to do. That's kinda' hard for some people to swallow. But listen, I don't mean to offend you no ways, but to be real, listen, I get pissed on by a better class of white people than you. Yeah…I do.

(takes a breath)

VINCENT. *(cont.)* And you know what? It's been a long day. So let's just call it quits for now.

(He pushes a button on an intercom and speaks into it.)

My client needs an escort from the interview room, please.

EVELYN. Pook is my daughter.

VINCENT. Christina?

EVELYN. Yes.

VINCENT. Okay. I presume you want to see her again. Yes?

(She snorts.)

I'll take that as a yes. You have no shoelaces. You on a watch?

EVELYN. Yeah.

VINCENT. Don't go and do anything stupid all right?

EVELYN. I ain't gonna off myself.

VINCENT. Good. You owe your daughter that.

EVELYN. Don't you tell me what to do, faggot!

VINCENT. *(He cuts her off before she gets the word out.)* Here you go again. Stop shooting yourself in the foot, you are going to have plenty of folks that will do that for you.

*(**EVELYN** snorts again.)*

Hey, how about words for a starter. This snorting thing ain't gonna go down in court. You got a sinus condition or something?

EVELYN. No.

VINCENT. You just think about what I said. Figure it out, okay. Figure it out.

(He pushes the button on the intercom again.)

Guard!

*(to **EVELYN**)*

Don't talk to no one in here.

(pushing button again)

Guard!!

EVELYN. Could you... I think I should be allowed to call...

(She looks away.)

VINCENT. *(waiting)* You want to talk to Christina?

EVELYN. Yeah.

VINCENT. Okay. All right. I can hook you up with a phone call.

EVELYN. Promise?

VINCENT. Yeah. Most definitely. I'll hook you up.

*(Lights fade out as **VINCENT** moves quickly away from the interview room.)*

Scene Three

*(**VINCENT** walks into another space as lights shift. He is now in the lobby of the building housing the office of the Public Defenders. **MAIA**, walking in from another direction, carries a load of briefs. From nearby, we hear protesters shouting, "Justice for Baby David. Justice for Baby David.")*

VINCENT. *(stopping her before she can speak)* I'm not ready to make a statement.

MAIA. It might help. Public opinion could sink us. You represent a lot to the people of this county. Seeing your face on local TV –

VINCENT. I'm not showing my face yet. Okay?

MAIA. Fine. They're going for murder?

VINCENT. Murder One.

MAIA. Have you devised a strategy?

VINCENT. I'm still looking at the evidence.

MAIA. What about her state of mind?

VINCENT. I'm not sure how depressed she is. She rallied enough to get all racist and high-handed with me.

MAIA. Jailhouse puffery. Everyone who gives birth has some form of blues or blahs or something.

VINCENT. Maybe.

MAIA. Imagine passing a kidney stone the size of a bowling ball. Without an epidural!

VINCENT. I guess most women survive –

MAIA. Then a day after the blessed ordeal is over, the hospital kicks you out so you have to go back to a house that had fallen into ruin as a result of your supposedly joyful excursion into biology and modern obstetrics –

VINCENT. *(thrown in)* Okay, okay. Got it –

MAIA. Don't interrupt. Then nature gives you a final kick. The hormones take a free-fall nosedive. And suddenly you are tending to a colicky baby and wiping a shriveled up poopy bottom, sure that your life is over and singing Joni Mitchell tunes until your husband is ready to wring your neck.

VINCENT. Not to be rude –

MAIA. And when you finally have the nerve to leave the house and go to the grocery store, the check-out girl looks at your belly that won't go down even after you've dropped a nine-pound baby. And when she asks, "So when's the baby due?" That's when you want to take a soldering iron and cauterize your fallopian tubes!

VINCENT. I'm not sure I am ready for this level –

MAIA. And that's the nice middle-class scenario. Add to that all the other stuff that this young woman was facing, what is her name, Evelyn? A small child to tend to besides the baby, miserable living conditions! Come on, Vincent. Use your imagination!

VINCENT. I do have a mother, you know.

MAIA. So I understand.

VINCENT. She had to deal with all the shit this woman was facing. My dad died just after Naomi was born. She was living on a pittance, raising four kids.

MAIA. I know that your mother had it tough. She lived through some difficult –

VINCENT. And she didn't get herself into the mess this girl is in.

MAIA. Good for her. She was lucky.

VINCENT. Luck had nothing to do with it. She had a will and a notion of how she was determined to live. That's what she had.

MAIA. Well, this girl didn't have that?

VINCENT. No, I don't think so.

MAIA. How many of your clients have had that?

VINCENT. What?

MAIA. A will and a notion of how they are determined to live.

VINCENT. I don't know.

MAIA. Not many.

VINCENT. Maybe not.

(There is the sound of a hymn sung by a group of people. Unaccompanied. Rough and amateurish.)

MAIA. Oh shit, I'm due back in court in a half hour and I'm going to have to break through a prayer circle.

(pause)

After what…four, almost five years in this office, you still want things to be simple.

VINCENT. Yes, I do. I'm just a simple country boy.

MAIA. Okay, country boy. What have you got for me?

VINCENT. I have some character witnesses. Her daughter's teacher says she is a passable mother to Christina. Her boss at the supermarket says she was a tough cookie but dead honest and hard working. We have no evidence that she's a druggie, she steered clear of all that, but she drinks. She has a prior arrest, a DUI and we have Jack Hoover, her neighbor who says she was drinking pretty heavily the night of David's death.

MAIA. Did they do a blood alcohol at her arraignment?

VINCENT. No.

MAIA. Any record of child abuse?

VINCENT. Uh, uh.

MAIA. Nothing with child protective services?

VINCENT. Nothing.

MAIA. Okay. The father?

VINCENT. He is out of state with a strong alibi. Oh, kind of a downer. A big downer, actually. Investigators said she showed a lack of emotion when she reported her child missing.

MAIA. Oh, dear. No one likes a stoic mother.

VINCENT. I'm afraid not.

MAIA. Stoic father is fine. Stoic mother. That's a no-no.

(pause)

Have you gotten her version of events yet?

VINCENT. No. Not really.

MAIA. You are giving the prosecutor's office plenty of time to prepare a rock solid case?

VINCENT. I can't just plow into her. She's a cactus!

MAIA. This could be big, Vincent. People are going to be writing about it. Conservatives, feminists, the lot!

VINCENT. I am not the only person who is having a hard time with this.

MAIA. A few fanatics waving posters at the courthouse are unnerving you? Come on!

VINCENT. Some of those fanatics are my people out there. Not some neo-Nazi, Ku Klux Klan wannabes.

MAIA. So some of them are black, is that what's bothering you?

VINCENT. Well it's less fun when the person calling you an Antichrist baptized you.

MAIA. You are not the local hero anymore?

VINCENT. My mother isn't talking to me.

MAIA. She'll get over it.

(pause)

Your client is poor, a racist pain in the ass and she could be a dicey mother. She still needs to be defended from people ready to chuck jurisprudence just so that they can forget that women like her exist.

(Vincent's cell phone rings.)

MAIA. *(cont.)* If that's another headhunter, tell them to keep their claws out of you, country boy, I need you in this office!

VINCENT. *(looking at the number)* It's my sister, my sister!

MAIA. Okay!

VINCENT. *(talking into the phone)* Hey Naomi…Oh, no!

(He puts his hand over the phone. To **MAIA***, whispering:)*

Sorry, Maia.

MAIA. Everything all right?

VINCENT. It's just family shit. But I gotta' take it.

MAIA. I know from family shit. Take it. Take it. I'm gone.

(She leaves.)

VINCENT. *(speaking into the phone)* Easy, Naomi. I'll track him down.

(He starts to put on his suit coat.)

Oh, Naomi…don't tell Mama, okay? I mean, he may just be, you know…hanging out. Thanks.

(He hangs up the phone and looks out into space seeing something.)

Ray! You reckless bastard!

Scene Four

(As **VINCENT** *stands lost in thought lights come up on* **RAY** *now 13, standing on a train trestle.* **VINCENT***, turns and looks up at him and becomes dizzy.)*

RAY. What you call me?

VINCENT. *(hopping out of life in the now, enters into memory, finding his way toward the train trestle[*])* You are a crazy, reckless bastard!

---

[*]The actor playing Vincent can turn his back and place a magnetized emblem on his blazer to create a private school uniform.

RAY. *(laughing)* Look at you. It's the motherfucking FBI.

(cowering)

Don't shoot! Don't shoot!

VINCENT. Shut up. Come on! Get down.

RAY. That the monkey suit they put you in at the academy?

VINCENT. Yeah, what of it?

RAY. *(losing it, hysterical)* Oh shit!

VINCENT. *(slipping into his adolescent self)* It's a uniform. Everyone wears it!

RAY. At least you fit in with the rest of them freaks.

VINCENT. Okay fine. Just get down.

RAY. Just cause you goin' to that phoneyass place where all the preppie freaks thinks they better –

VINCENT. Mama made me –

RAY. – don't you think you gonna' start schooling me.

VINCENT. God, no, who would try to school –

RAY. You may be the book learner in the family but that don't mean you ain't stupid!

VINCENT. Of course, Ray, sure! I'm stupid.

RAY. Just so you know.

VINCENT. No, Ray, everyone knows I'm stupid and you're the genius in the family.

RAY. Yeah, that's right!

VINCENT. You're so smart you don't even have to go to school, huh?

RAY. Don't get cute on me and shit!

VINCENT. Come on, Ray. It's starting to get dark. Let's go home.

RAY. Nah!

VINCENT. Mama's going nuts! The washer died again and Carrie has another one of her earaches. Mama was cussin! And you know what that means!

RAY. *(letting his mask slip for a second)* She care so much, whyn't she come looking?

VINCENT. She's tired running after you!

RAY. So I will do what I want.

(looking him over)

Look at you, hunkering down. Stand up, ya sissie!

VINCENT. No thanks. I don't want to fall.

RAY. You ain't gonna fall.

(taking his arm)

Come on, I got you. Straighten up! Open your eyes.

VINCENT. Don't touch me! Don't –

(He opens his eyes. Tentatively, he looks down.)

Look at that! There's our house, looking like a piece on a monopoly board!

RAY. Yeah!

VINCENT. Down there with Mama on top of us…you forget there's all this.

RAY. Life don't begin and end with our 3/4 acre of land.

VINCENT. I guess not.

(They pause for a moment, looking out. **VINCENT** *sees something.)*

Is that the paper mill over there near the dump?

RAY. *(looking away)* Uh-huh.

VINCENT. *(after a moment)* Hey man, where do you go when you take off? You don't just sleep on a trestle.

RAY. I've got friends.

VINCENT. Were you with your friends when Mama told me you were at Aunt Rose's in Turnbeck?

RAY. *(touching his bandaged arms)* I was with Aunt Rose. Always have me runnin' after her dentucreme and shit –

VINCENT. Mmmmmm. I don't think so.

RAY. Oh yeah? What you think, smartass?

VINCENT. I don't know, Ray. Things changed after you went away that time. Something happened.

RAY. Nothing happened. Ain't nothing going on in Turnbeck.

VINCENT. Some of the kids have been saying things –

RAY. What they saying?

VINCENT. About those people who live in the paper mill.

RAY. *(suddenly his volatile side fires up)* Tell those motherfuckers to shut the hell up!!!

VINCENT. *(frightened of this side of his brother)* I'll tell them, Ray.

RAY. I'll beat the shit out of them, you understand?

VINCENT. You'll kick some asses! I'll tell them, shut the hell up.

(The sound of a train in the distance.)

Ray, look! We got to get off this trestle now!!!

RAY. Fuck the train. I ain't moving!

VINCENT. Ray!!! Come on.

(starting to leave)

Jesus Christ, I'm getting down. You can get yourself killed.

*(**VINCENT** starts to move toward one end of the tracks where he can get off and **RAY** grabs his arm.)*

RAY. *(has gotten himself into a bad place)* Come on, don't leave me just as all the fun is going to start. Come on, boy. Show me what you got.

*(**VINCENT** tries to break free as the sound of the train gets louder. **RAYMOND** pulls him down. They begin to wrestle. **RAY** is laughing. **VINCENT** is angry and scared.)*

VINCENT. Let me go!

*(**VINCENT** takes a slug at **RAY**. **RAY** laughs.)*

RAY. Is that your best? That all you got?

(They wrestle some more, panting and groaning. The train sounds become more insistent.)

VINCENT. *(starts to cry)* Jesus, Ray. We're going to die!

RAY. *(Looking over his shoulder. Realizes he has taken it too far.)* Oh shit! Stop fighting and just hold onto me. I know what to do!

VINCENT. No you don't! You'll kill both of us!

RAY. Stop it.

VINCENT. LET GO!!!!

RAY. Hold on. I know where to stand and let the train pass!

(He maneuvers the two of them onto a cross beam that extends out from the tracks. VINCENT gasps as the train approaches.)

Breathe.

VINCENT. *(crying)* Why did you get us into this?

RAY. Settle down, now. It'll pass. I'm holding on, little brother. Holding on to you.

(RAY locks VINCENT in an embrace and pushes him against an unseen structure. A strobe indicates the passing of a train.)

Scene Five

(When the lights come back up again VINCENT is standing with his jacket in hand in the interview room in the county jail. EVELYN has just entered and she regards VINCENT who is struggling to get his breath.)

EVELYN. What's wrong?

VINCENT. What?

EVELYN. You're breathing like your gonna' die.

VINCENT. I'm – I'm – I walked up the stairs. It's nothing. Nothing.

EVELYN. Elevator out of order?

VINCENT. I don't take elevators.

EVELYN. You're strange.

VINCENT. *(Taking a notebook and pen out of a briefcase. Trying to get his breathing under control.)* Okay, I don't have much time. Let's get moving on this. The prosecution is going to try and depict you as someone who doesn't – someone who has some ambivalence – some mixed feelings –

EVELYN. I'm a good mother.

VINCENT. Can we prove that to a jury?

(She is silent. He reads from a notebook.)

Your neighbor says you told him on the afternoon before David died that you were ready to "kill the fucking brats."

EVELYN. *(snapping)* What?

VINCENT. *(unswerving)* That's what he said.

EVELYN. Liar!

VINCENT. Really?

EVELYN. Well…I don't remember everything I say. Do you?

VINCENT. If you take the stand, we can't fudge the truth and we can't let ourselves get eaten alive by the prosecution.

EVELYN. I want my daughter back.

VINCENT. So.

(pause, then forcefully)

Did you say it?

EVELYN. I didn't mean it.

VINCENT. *(firmly)* But you said it.

EVELYN. There was no heat in the apartment. The washer wasn't working.

VINCENT. So you are saying you said it. I just want to be clear.

EVELYN. You stay at home all day in one room with two – Don't tell me your mother never said things like that when she was strung out!

VINCENT. I don't remember.

EVELYN. See?

VINCENT. See what?

EVELYN. Forget it.

VINCENT. You better think about how you gonna' answer that, Evelyn.

(He takes out a pad and gets back to business. The next questions are asked quickly, much as a doctor does an initial intake.)

Social services says that you refused to identify the baby's father when you gave birth?

EVELYN. That's right.

VINCENT. Okay. Do you have a relationship with this man?

EVELYN. No.

VINCENT. Is he Christina's father as well?

EVELYN. No. Her father's in prison. We haven't spoken in three years. Their fathers aren't even in the state.

VINCENT. So fine. Let's leave them out of this. Okay. Did your caseworker ever pay you any visits?

EVELYN. No, they said at the hospital, they were going to come out to see my new apartment, but they didn't.

VINCENT. *(looks up from his writing)* So this was a new place for you and the children?

EVELYN. Yeah. We moved because the old place was condemned after the flood.

VINCENT. And this new place was supposed to be an improvement?

EVELYN. Yeah.

*(**EVELYN** gets up and starts to move around the room, pushing up against the walls with various parts of her body like a cat.)*

VINCENT. *(noting her discomfort)* You need a glass of water or anything?

EVELYN. I'm okay.

VINCENT. Okay. Let's keep going. When was the last time you saw David?

EVELYN. When I went to bed.

VINCENT. And that was?

EVELYN. About 11 o'clock.

VINCENT. He was asleep by then?

EVELYN. Yeah.

VINCENT. When had you put him to bed?

EVELYN. Nine o'clock or so.

VINCENT. How did he seem? Did he go to bed easily?

EVELYN. He was fussy that night.

VINCENT. So…did you soothe him?

EVELYN. Sure I did.

VINCENT. *(considers for a moment)* Did you…breast-feed him?

(EVELYN stops moving and turns around to face him. Looks at him for a minute.)

EVELYN. I don't know where that is any of your business.

VINCENT. Evelyn, it is something that someone is going to ask. Might as well settle our version of events now.

EVELYN. Well, all right, then. Yes, I tried.

VINCENT. You tried?

EVELYN. Yeah, but he didn't suck right. Not like Christina. He never liked to suck. He would suck for a few seconds. That was all.

VINCENT. So why didn't you call your doctor?

EVELYN. He wasn't sick. He was fussy. I gave him a bottle.

(She looks down. A stain is spreading across her chest.)

Oh Jesus! I'm letting down.

VINCENT. What?

EVELYN. My breast milk is still – I'm leaking! Don't you know anything? Do you have a handkerchief? Some tissues?

VINCENT. Here.

(He gives her some tissues and then turns his back as she stuffs them in her bra. She then stands with her hands folded across her chest.)

We can take a breather.

EVELYN. I'll be all right. It stopped.

(pause)

Weird thing is I deliver milk like a garden hose. I could feed ten. But he didn't suck at me.

(collecting herself)

EVELYN. So yeah, I gave him a bottle.

VINCENT. Did he drink?

EVELYN. Yeah. A little. Enough that it made him drowsy.

VINCENT. And then he went to sleep?

EVELYN. Yeah, and then I put Christina down, too.

VINCENT. And you went outside?

EVELYN. I sat on my stoop.

VINCENT. What were you doing there? Wasn't it cold?

EVELYN. I don't know. Just had to get out.

VINCENT. Try to recall.

EVELYN. Just looking at the sky. Thinking.

VINCENT. Anything else?

EVELYN. No. That's all.

VINCENT. Were you drinking anything? Eating?

EVELYN. Ate a slim jim.

VINCENT. And nothing else?

EVELYN. No.

VINCENT. *(prodding)* You sure?

EVELYN. Yeah.

VINCENT. *(Sighing. She is a liar.)* So when did you come in?

EVELYN. I guess it was about 11 o'clock.

VINCENT. And you went to bed right away?

EVELYN. No, I cleaned up a little. We had a party for Christina. She turned five. I took down some balloons and crepe paper.

VINCENT. Okay. And then?

EVELYN. I washed up and all.

VINCENT. Uh huh.

EVELYN. Said my prayers.

VINCENT. Oh. Do you go to Church?

EVELYN. Nah.

VINCENT. But you pray.

EVELYN. Sometimes.

VINCENT. This is hard to ask…but it's something I know will be asked if you take the stand.

(He takes a deep breath and swallows.)

Did you…did you want this baby?

EVELYN. *(sharply)* Why are you asking me that?

VINCENT. *(quickly, attempting to mitigate his misfire)* You were in a tough way, Evelyn. No partner, no maternity leave from your job, a five year-old to manage –

EVELYN. *(softly)* You think I killed him, don't you?

VINCENT. No, I don't. But, it would be understandable if you had some mixed feelings –

EVELYN. *(gaining force)* I didn't kill my son!

VINCENT. No one is –

(letting his frustration show)

It's just that we have to know how that baby came to be lying in a bean field. That baby got there somehow. Now maybe you had too much to drink –

EVELYN. *(overlapping)* I could have had an abortion.

(yelling)

They fucking begged me…they almost paid me to have one.

(She looks at her chest.)

Oh, God, I'm letting down again –

VINCENT. Evelyn, take it easy, now –

EVELYN. No one wants a poor bitch like me to have kids!! They think I'm too stupid to take care of them –

VINCENT. No one says that you are stupid, no one –

EVELYN. Why would I go through the fucking 24 hours of hard labor to have a kid I didn't want, you dumb faggot –

VINCENT. Evelyn, calm down –

(She knocks down her chair.)

EVELYN. My son is dead; my daughter is living with people I don't even know –

VINCENT. Come on, Evelyn. I'm on your side. Do you think I want to lose a case?

EVELYN. I don't do drugs –

(She kicks a chair. It falls to the ground.)

VINCENT. No one says you do drugs –

EVELYN. I don't fuck around. I just want to live like a normal person with my kids!!!

VINCENT. Evelyn, calm down, now!

EVELYN. Calm down? Calm down! Jesus Christ, can't you just do your job and get me the hell out of here!

(As she speaks she begins pounding on the door that is locked. Then she begins hitting her head against the wall, pushing down chairs, etc.)

Get me the hell out of here!!! Get me out!! Get me out!!!

Scene Six

*(Lights come down on the interview room as **VINCENT** walks into **RITA**'s living room. **RITA** sits on the couch. Her feet are propped up on a cushion. Her knee is bandaged. On another part of the stage, **RAY** sits at a table. He is preparing to shoot up some heroin. Lighting effects indicate that **RAY** is not physically present in the scene with **RITA** and **VINCENT** but rather exists as a psychic projection of **VINCENT**'s anxieties about his family.)*

RITA. *(breathing heavily)* I came back into the living room and he was there. Sweat pouring out of him. Eyes starting out of his head –

VINCENT. How did he get in? Wasn't the door locked?

RITA. He was all in my purse –

VINCENT. Damn!

RITA. I said, "Ray, what you doing here? It's Saturday. You supposed to be watching Naomi's kids." He said he was just going to borrow some money. I told him to get out of my purse. But he pushed me down when I tried to get it from him.

VINCENT. Oh, God!

RITA. I twisted my knee.

VINCENT. Why do you tussle with him when he's in this state?

RITA. I told him I was going to call the police on him.

VINCENT. Never say that when he's like this. He's dangerous!

RITA. When I picked up the phone, he ran away with my purse.

VINCENT. With all your ID?

RITA. Social Security. Everything.

VINCENT. I'll get on the phone.

RITA. Naomi will be back with the kids in a few minutes. They're gonna spend the night.

VINCENT. He's got to be in a program.

RITA. I called the police! I don't care about a program. He needs to be behind bars.

VINCENT. *(to RITA)* That won't help.

RITA. Yeah? It will help me! It will help this family. Those kids were alone in the house while Naomi was at work! He was hitting up in Naomi's shed! They found all sorts of stuff he uses. The kids found it. The kids! I can't live like this. Scared to open the door to my own son. I pressed charges and there is a warrant out for his arrest.

VINCENT. Oh, come on, Mama. He's sick!

RITA. And once they pick him up, don't go raising bail and pulling strings for him like you're always doing.

VINCENT. *(His face is tightening.)* Look, I know you are angry, but –

RITA. Don't look at me like that.

VINCENT. But I don't want to hang him out to dry!

RITA. Fine. Leave it to me. I'll hang him out to dry. That man is gonna' kill me.

VINCENT. He won't get any help in the system. He comes out worse off than when he goes in.

RITA. That's not my problem.

VINCENT. He hasn't had it easy, Mama.

RITA. Too easy. That's his problem.

VINCENT. I don't think –

RITA. He was brought up same as you. Had the same opportunities.

VINCENT. It was different with me.

RITA. Yeah it was different. You worked! Had some respect for your elders –

VINCENT. Yeah, but it was easier for me.

RITA. How was it easier?

VINCENT. I was a different kid. People liked me. Teachers, adults…they favored me.

RITA. And why was that?

VINCENT. I don't know why.

RITA. Ray isn't dumb. He could have had the same.

VINCENT. But he didn't. He couldn't. He had problems. Maybe even a mood disorder of some kind –

RITA. Mood disorder! Lack of will power!

VINCENT. Maybe if you had the time when he was growing up –

RITA. *(jumping to the defensive)* What?

VINCENT. It's just that –

RITA. Yeah?

VINCENT. You were so busy with the others –

RITA. I was the same to all my children –

VINCENT. And there were times when he got so wild and you didn't –

*(Suddenly **RAY** looks up from what he has been doing, sober and dead serious.)*

RAY. Shut up, Vincent.

RITA. What?

VINCENT. You were going to the emergency room every other day with all my allergies –

RITA. So?

VINCENT. And he ran the neighborhood. And there was that crowd at the paper mill. And you just –

RAY. I said shut the fuck up, you little punk. Leave the old lady alone.

VINCENT. When he was gone that time – He came home, he was filthy. Was he with Aunt Rose?

RAY. Don't go digging up that shit –

RITA. What are you talking about?

VINCENT. His teacher brought me into a room and she wanted to know –

RAY. *(suddenly sad and childlike)* Vincent, buddy, I don't want to go there.

RITA. *(suddenly at attention)* A teacher? At his school?

RAY. Let it go, huh? Come on, little brother. Don't take me there, please baby.

RITA. Ray got in trouble with the teacher?

VINCENT. No, that's not what –

*(**RAY** rolls up his sleeves and looks at some burn marks on his arms that are raw and red. He raises his arms. His scars seemed to brighten into a stigmata.)*

RAY. Oh my God, throw me away!

VINCENT. He was thirteen, Mom. He was –

RAY. *(screaming)* LEAVE IT BE!

(quietly)

You're fucking up my high.

(Everyone is still for a moment.)

VINCENT. Forget about it.

RAY. *(quietly)* Yeah, forget about it.

RITA. Vincent, listen to me now. You got to take care of your own life.

VINCENT. *(wearily, to **RITA**)* I live my life.

RITA. Between that awful job you have and running after Ray! You don't have a minute to take stock of things.

RAY. That's the idea.

RITA. Vincent, you could do anything you want. You could walk into just about any law office, anywhere and be hired. Public defense! They don't pay you anything –

VINCENT. Let's not get into this –

RAY. Yeah, let's not get into it!

RITA. They have you working crazy hours, running from pillar to post.

VINCENT. I'm not unhappy –

RAY. But you ain't flying, are you?

RITA. You could be making a good living.

RAY. You need freedom to fly.

VINCENT. Mom, I have a good job.

RITA. Yeah, you like going to bat for a woman who killed her baby?

RAY. Oh, you'll never fly with that mill stone around your neck.

VINCENT. Mom, leave it!

RITA. Where is the justice in that?

RAY. You just a mill stone collector, ain't you!

VINCENT. We don't know –

RITA. That's some way to use a college education. That's all I got to say about that.

VINCENT. *(to both of them)* Get off my back!

(He calms down a bit.)

I'm sorry, Mama. Ray is off. He's gone. He could just go flying out of the earth's orbit for all we know.

RITA. And there is nothing that we can do about it.

*(**RAY** has shot up and he slowly unwinds. He sings an old hymn and it continues until the end of the scene.)*

RAY.

JUST AS I AM, WITHOUT ONE PLEA,
BUT THAT THY BLOOD WAS SHED FOR ME,

VINCENT. I can't believe that.

RITA. He's not gonna take me down. No way. Uh, uh. I gave enough of the marrow of my good days. Yes, indeed. Just about killed me.

(pause)

I have to live. That's what I have to do.

RAY. *(singing under the ensuing dialogue, starting and stopping without regard for time)*

AND THAT THOU BIDST ME COME TO THEE,

O LAMB OF GOD, I COME, I COME.

RITA. *(looks at* **VINCENT***)* So now what you gonna do, huh? How you gonna fix this mess? Hmmmm. *(bitterly)* You're going to save your big brother, that it? All the drug counselors, doctors, social workers…they couldn't do nothing. What are you gonna' do?

*(***VINCENT*** turns to look at* **RAY***.)*

RAY.

JUST AS I AM, THOUGH TOSSED ABOUT

WITH MANY A CONFLICT, MANY A DOUBT,

FIGHTINGS AND FEARS WITHIN, WITHOUT,

O LAMB OF GOD, I COME, I COME.**

Scene Seven

(As **RAY** *sings lights come up on an abandoned bean field on the edge of town. Shadows of the railroad trestle play against the ground. A makeshift shrine is loaded with stuffed animals, crosses, notes to baby David.* **VINCENT** *walks into the field and joins* **MAIA***. He pauses looking up as though hearing* **RAY***'s song.)*

MAIA. This isn't farmed anymore?

*(***VINCENT*** doesn't answer.)*

Vincent?

** Words: Charlotte Elliott, 1835. Music: William Bradbury, 1849

VINCENT. Sorry. Ahhh...I don't think so. They moved south a few years back after the canneries closed.

MAIA. *(after a moment)* She's still standing by her story?

VINCENT. Yes, she put the baby to bed and when she woke up and discovered he was missing, she called 911.

MAIA. Any other suspects?

VINCENT. No.

MAIA. You got the the autopsy report?

VINCENT. *(handing it to her and waving his arms)* Bugs all over this place.

MAIA. Only 6 and 3/4 pounds! After what? 22 days!

VINCENT. The coroner fixes time of death between 3 and 4 in the morning. The baby was discovered here at 8:30. Asphyxiation.

(pause)

There is something else that was discovered in the autopsy. The baby had a congenital heart defect.

MAIA. Really?

VINCENT. If David had lived, would have needed treatment, maybe surgery –

MAIA. And this was not diagnosed at the hospital when Evelyn gave birth?

VINCENT. No. But Evelyn told me the baby wasn't sucking. And he hadn't put on weight. So I asked the medical examiner to make sure the autopsy was thorough and they picked it up.

MAIA. Nice catch!

(thinking strategy now)

This finding might help you. You could claim this condition made the baby more vulnerable to accidental suffocation or even Sudden Infant. But it could also hurt you.

VINCENT. How?

MAIA. Prosecution will suggest that she knew that the baby would have problems. Problems she was ill-equipped to handle. And from there they will make the leap that she was practicing a form of eugenics.

VINCENT. How could she see this condition when a qualified practitioner hadn't –

MAIA. She might have known something was amiss. She has raised a girl. She knows what a healthy baby is like. David did not put on weight. He wasn't sucking.

VINCENT. So you think –

MAIA. You must entertain all of the possibilities. Mothers do all sorts of things that people don't want to think about. We practice triage, you know.

VINCENT. Triage?

MAIA. Yes. A mother has a pile of chips. Let's say the chips are her money, her time and whatever other resources she can squirrel away. She looks at her pile of chips and she decides not only which of her children needs them but also which of her children is most likely to return her investment.

VINCENT. That's kind of cold.

MAIA. Nature is cold. You get women alone in a room and most of them will tell you, if they are honest, that they had moments when they felt cold toward their newborn. I remember looking at my newborn like he was a mutant or something. I was young and scared, new

MAIA. *(cont.)* to the country. And it got worse when the others came because then I had all these decisions to make about which one would get what. Can't you see this in your own upbringing?

VINCENT. Not particularly.

MAIA. How many of your siblings went to college?

VINCENT. Just me.

MAIA. So why is that? Why out of four kids brought up in the same environment are you the only one with a degree? Are the others incapable?

VINCENT. *(on the edge of testy)* No.

MAIA. Then why?

VINCENT. I don't know.

MAIA. You don't think your mother made a few decisions about who she was going to push forward and of course when you push one forward then the others –

VINCENT. You know, Maia…I know where this conversation is going and I don't like it. I have to defend this woman. It's my job. But don't try to sell me on some Darwinian bull shit. I am not basing a defense on that. This is not the Stone Age. Women don't have the right to decide which of their children is worth keeping alive!

MAIA. Of course not!

VINCENT. *(sharply)* And don't use my mother to defend your third world theories –

MAIA. Excuse me –

VINCENT. My mother broke her back to give all of her kids a good life and I don't –

MAIA. *(chastened)* I am sure she did. I didn't mean –

VINCENT. She had it every bit as hard as this young woman. Trust me!

MAIA. You're angry with her, aren't you?

VINCENT. *(quickly)* Who, my mother?

MAIA. No, Evelyn!

VINCENT. Oh please, give me a little credit here.

MAIA. You think she didn't love that baby.

VINCENT. *(flustered)* Well, I've started to consider that. Anyone would.

MAIA. All right. Good. Let's go there. Say she didn't love this baby. Suppose that with all that she was up against, the love that she was supposed to feel for this child wasn't there – at least in any consistent way.

VINCENT. You're excusing her.

MAIA. Mother love isn't some hard commodity. It's fragile! No one wants to admit that! Oh God, people are so damn benighted and you are about the worst!!

(She pauses. He just looks at her.)

VINCENT. Thanks!

MAIA. How are you?

VINCENT. I'm fine.

MAIA. Any word from Ray?

VINCENT. No. Did you hear from any of your connections?

MAIA. No. Sorry. Not a peep.

VINCENT. Shit!

MAIA. Really, Vincent, are you okay?

VINCENT. *(after a moment)* I don't want to go to trial, Maia.

MAIA. What?

VINCENT. I want to negotiate a plea. I don't think they have enough to get Murder One. They'll come back with something. I'll present her with a good deal.

MAIA. I'm lost.

VINCENT. I don't want to put that woman on the stand! She's a dead bang loser, a lying drunk who tantrums like a two year-old. The weird ticks! And the racism! She's not even smart enough to hide it from the sucker of color, that would be me, who's trying to get her off. Jesus Christ! Do you really want to put me through that! You know the jury pool we get. They'll hate her.

MAIA. So let's move for a change of venue.

VINCENT. We'll never get a change of venue and the way this trial is being covered we will have alienated the community even more.

MAIA. God forbid you stand apart from your community!

VINCENT. I have some loyalty to my community. Yes, I do. I stand here because of them.

MAIA. You know, you could win this case!

VINCENT. Oh come on, Maia!

MAIA. Seriously, she could walk or at least get off for time served. It's a little tricky, but you've argued worse. What have they got? Some busybody who says she drinks. An eighty year-old male psychologist who doesn't like the fact that she didn't cry when she reported her child missing! There are no substantial witnesses! No clear cause of death established! I don't get it.

VINCENT. Yeah, go ahead. Put my neck on the chopping block!

MAIA. Vincent. Are you going to leave this office?

VINCENT. What?

MAIA. It's been just about five years since you started.

VINCENT. So?

MAIA. Do you know how many kids I've seen jump off at the five year point? You are starting to act like someone who's getting ready to jump.

VINCENT. I've served the office. People do other things. They have homes, hobbies, memberships in country clubs.

MAIA. Don't bull shit me! This office needs you and you know it. I won't be here forever. I don't want to hand things over to some kid who is just clocking in a few years to rack up trial time and connections.

VINCENT. Well, I may not be the one, Maia.

MAIA. So, all right, maybe you will leave me. Fine. It's happened before. I'll go on. I'm a lifer. But don't think you are going to ease your way into a big city law firm with some half-assed plea bargain. Not under my watch. No way.

(She looks at him.)

Something about this case, something about this woman is getting under your skin. But I won't let you run from that and go for a plea.

VINCENT. Just who do you think I am, Maia?

MAIA. I think you can defend this woman. You are closer to her than you think. Trust yourself, Vincent. Use yourself. Use your history. It will bring you to this girl.

VINCENT. What if I don't want to go there?

MAIA. Fine. It's your life. Join the country club. They're taking people of color now.

(*She collects her things.*)

There is something we are leaving out or this conversation. Something big.

VINCENT. *(baffled)* What?

MAIA. You saw her apartment back there. Anything unusual?

VINCENT. *(suddenly)* I don't know, just the basic, section eight, make-shift –

MAIA. My God, you are such a man. There was no crib for the baby. No crib. No bassinet, no cradle.

VINCENT. So they were all sleeping in one single bed. All three of them!

MAIA. There is a story here, Vincent.

VINCENT. I'll take another shot with her.

MAIA. *(lightly)* Suit yourself.

(*The sound of a whistle. She looks up at the train trestle.*)

Whenever you see a train trestle in a movie, you know there is gonna' be trouble. A murder, suicide, kids getting into shit. What is that?

VINCENT. Don't know.

MAIA. You got your car?

VINCENT. Yeah.

MAIA. All right. Look sharp, Counselor.

(*She leaves.*)

Scene Eight

(**VINCENT** *walks around taking in the scene, he bends down, looks at something, throws it over his shoulder. Then he stands looking up at the train trestle. His breathing deepens and then lights change and* **RAY** *steps into the gridwork shadows of the train trestle. As* **RAY** *speaks lights come up on the Heffernon living room.* **RITA** *enters with her Bible. She stands at a window, looking out.*)

RAY. I was lying down under the back porch on a bed of dried leaves looking out through a crack in the boards, listening to her calling me as she leaned out the back door.

RITA. *(softly)* Raymond Wilson Heffernon, where are you!!!

(RITA stands lost in thought as though she is being visited by her errant son, haunted by his memory.)

RAY. She came out on the porch carrying my little brother who was then a colicky, testy little runt. Even in her scuffs, her foot landed heavy on the boards above me, blockin' out the thread of sunlight that came through. She was so close that I could hear the sound of her rubber hose whinin' as her thighs worked together.
"Don't you hide from me, you little devil! Ain't had a thing to eat all day long."

(pause)

"I'm gonna count. One-two-three-four –"
She came down the stairs and walked out toward the barn we had in the back.

"You in that barn, Raymond? Don't make me get to ten –

RAY. *(contd., pause)* Five, six, seven – Don't make me – Ra-a-a-a-a-ay? Eight – I'm almost at ten, Ray. N-i-i-i-ne..."

(pause)

"Nine and a half –"

(pause)

RAY. *(cont.)* "All right I'm at ten, now."
I saw her coming back toward the house. Walking in circles and bending down to check under the bee balm and behind the trash cans.

"Okay, that's it. I ain't gonna look for you no more. Cause you don't want to be looked for. That's all there is to that. I am going to leave you to the gypsies. The gypsies know what to do with you. The gypsies will take you and make you shine up their pans all day long. You gonna' live in a tent. Eat the scrap food that fall off the table 'long with the dogs! You'll soon get tired of that life! But that's what you want and that's what you'll get trying to get the best of me, little vagabond. Goodbye and good riddance!"

She walked up to the porch again and took one last look around the yard. Then she went in slamming the door so hard my ears popped.

(pause.)

I wanted it to last longer, this feeling of power, but I knew that I was right on the razor's edge of my mother's dark side and I didn't want the day to go there. She would begin to panic or maybe even something worse. She might fall into a funk. And my mother's funk could flatten out the day like nothing else. So I slid out from my hiding place making sure that I made a big enough noise, when I pushed the garden hoe aside to get her attention in the kitchen. When she heard me, she yelped a little warrior cry and came running out to the back where I was hightailing it straight down to the crick. She knew where I was heading and she skipped down the hill, tearing past the lilac bush and on down through the grapevine trellis, kicking off her scuffs as she went. I started to laugh and she couldn't help herself; she started to laugh too.

*(**RITA** smiles.)*

And just before we got to the crick, I slowed up enough so that she could grab me by the edge of my T-shirt.

RITA. *(remembering how she once could command her son)* Gotcha'! No child of mine gonna' get the better of Miss Rita, uh-uh, no sir. I got you now, little mister. I gotcha'!

RAY. Her hair hung loose and damp. Heat came off of her mixed with the smell of Nivea. She must have put Vincent down for his nap because he wasn't riding her hip or toddling after her. Mr. B wasn't lurking in her shadow.

(pause)

I was alone with my mother.

(pause)

RAY. We studied each other hard by the side of that swollen creek. She dropped her arm. And for just a moment we slipped the bond of mother and son and we were just two people who were breathing together, slower and slower. In cool, out warm.

*(In the pause, **RITA** and **RAY** breathe together.)*

And then she remembered that I was her one living torment. And she pushed me hard up the hill, singing a song of the Israelites as she marched up behind me.

*(**RITA** shakes her head as though dismissing something and then lowers herself back into her chair and begins to pray silently rocking a little. Lights come down on her.)*

I ran away from my mother many times after that and she would come after me, sometimes cussin', sometimes laughing, sometimes grim and silent. But when I was thirteen, I ran away much farther than the far edge of our backyard. And that time my mother didn't come after me. And the gypsies got me just as my mother warned. But after seven days and seven nights, after I had seen more than I wanted to see of the world outside our 3/4 acre of land...I came home of my own accord.

*(Lights come down on **RAY**. **VINCENT** is left in a pool of light looking up at the train trestle.)*

End of Act I

ACT II

Scene 1

*(**VINCENT** and **EVELYN** are in the interview room. They are seated at a table and **VINCENT** has a pile of papers around him.)*

VINCENT. This is how we do it. I will be you.

EVELYN. How can you be me?

VINCENT. It's pretend. Role-playing. Just listen to me being you.

EVELYN. What's the point?

VINCENT. To help us get a handle on each other.

EVELYN. *(She leans back in her chair.)* I get you. But you don't get me.

VINCENT. Oh yeah?

EVELYN. Yeah.

VINCENT. Oh, I may not be as thick as all...

(changing his tack)

Well, you know what, maybe I am a little thick. You wouldn't be the first to take note of that. So maybe this could help me.

EVELYN. How does it work?

VINCENT. I have your statement to the police investigators.

(He hands it to her.)

Do you want to read it?

EVELYN. *(handing it back)* No. I know what I said.

VINCENT. I also brought some questions the prosecutors will ask and some statements made by some witnesses.

EVELYN. *(tries to grab the papers)* What the hell are people saying about me!!!!

VINCENT. We will get to that in just a minute. Relax.

EVELYN. I'm relaxed. I'm relaxed.

(grabbing at him again)

Let me see the motherfuckin' papers.

VINCENT. I will in time, Evelyn. But not till you calm down.

EVELYN. Okay.

VINCENT. *(He breathes in deeply.)* Now, I am going to tell your story. I'm just going to repeat the things that you said in this report and other things you have told me here in this room.

EVELYN. Yeah?

VINCENT. Then, I am going to put you in the power seat.

EVELYN. What?

VINCENT. You'll be the law.

EVELYN. How can I be the law?

VINCENT. You'll be the prosecutor. You'll listen to my story and try to figure out if it makes sense.

EVELYN. I think I could do that.

VINCENT. I think so, too. And I want you to be tough on me, Evelyn. Poke holes in the story when you can.

EVELYN. So I am being tough on myself, huh?

VINCENT. Yeah, actually, yeah.

EVELYN. Nothing new.

VINCENT. *(handing her a sheet)* I'm going to give you a little cheat sheet to kind of get you started in your role as prosecutor.

EVELYN. *(looking at the sheet)* These are things the other lawyers will ask me?

VINCENT. Right.

EVELYN. Okay.

VINCENT. Ready?

(**EVELYN** *nods.*)

So...I've taken the stand, sworn to tell the truth, etcetera, etcetera. Now you ask me the first question.

EVELYN. *(reading from a paper)* "Describe events as they occurred on the evening of March 16th."

VINCENT. I cleaned up some decorations from Christina's birthday party and made dinner around 6:30. After we ate, I did the dishes while Christina watched David.

VINCENT. *(cont.)* Then I gave David a bath in the kitchen sink.

(He pauses, checks in with her.)

Okay so far?

EVELYN. Okay. Keep going.

VINCENT. So then after the baby was bathed and put in his pajamas, I tried to feed him. First I tried– I tried to feed him using my breasts.

EVELYN. No one says it that way! Jesus! Say, "I nursed him!"

VINCENT. Okay. Okay. "I nursed him."

EVELYN. Better.

VINCENT. Thanks. But he wasn't sucking. He hadn't been sucking the last few days. So after I tried a few times, I gave up and I gave him a bottle.

(dropping out of his character)

How do I sound?

EVELYN. I believe you.

VINCENT. Good. So then he fell asleep and I put him to bed.

(**VINCENT** *waits for her response.*)

EVELYN. *(looking down at the paper)* Is it my turn?

(**VINCENT** *nods. She reads.*)

Where did you put David asleep?

VINCENT. He slept on the bed. A single bed. Where all three of us slept.

(pause)

VINCENT. Now come on, Evelyn. What would the prosecutor say to that?

EVELYN. I don't know.

VINCENT. Look on the sheet.

EVELYN. *(reading)* "Why didn't you put the baby in a crib or a bassinet or a cradle?"

VINCENT. I wanted to. But the one I had for Christina got ruined in storage when the basement was flooded the old house and I didn't have the money to buy another. And I didn't want to put him in a drawer on the floor because we had mice.

EVELYN. That's true.

(She gets up and starts to pace around the room.)

But, Jesus Christ, do you have to say that about my not having money?

VINCENT. I think its an important part of your story, Evelyn.

EVELYN. I worked my whole life, except for a few weeks after the babies were born and I don't want no one feeling sorry for me.

VINCENT. Why is it so bad for people to feel sorry for you?

EVELYN. You don't want people to feel sorry for you, do you?

VINCENT. No, I guess not–

EVELYN. You better than me?

VINCENT. I have had a different kind of life, that's all.

EVELYN. I have a right to my privacy –

VINCENT. You lost that right, Evelyn –

EVELYN. There you go. Just like the fuckin' cops!

VINCENT. Sorry, sorry. I lost my concentration. I forgot. I'm Evelyn. I'm Evelyn Laverty and I –

EVELYN. – don't want no one feeling sorry for me.

VINCENT. That's right. I don't want no one feeling sorry for me. But I am going to mention that social services made an agreement with me to get me some proper equipment for the baby. How's that?

EVELYN. That's okay. They fucked up.

VINCENT. I won't say it like that. I'll say. "They failed to live up to their promise."

EVELYN. That's true.

VINCENT. Next question.

EVELYN. What did you do after you put David to bed?

VINCENT. I cleaned up the apartment and helped Christina with some homework. I made her brush her teeth and clean up. She got into bed next to David and fell asleep.

EVELYN. I read her a story first!

VINCENT. Oh yeah! I read her a story. Sorry!

EVELYN. Whatever.

VINCENT. Then I went outside. I was tired and feeling a little shut in after a long day with the children. So I had a couple of beers and a cigarette to take the edge off.

EVELYN. Wait a minute! Wait a minute!

VINCENT. Evelyn, Counselor. I have some explaining to do here. People may be offended at the idea that a breast-feeding mother was drinking beer on a stoop.

EVELYN. So, don't mention it.

VINCENT. Jack Hoover is going to testify that you were getting plastered on your stoop after you put the kids to bed.

(He shows her a statement.)

Look!

EVELYN. What the fuck! Busybody!

VINCENT. He said he saw you drinking.

EVELYN. Two beers!

VINCENT. And smoking for that matter! And he says after the kids were asleep, some nights you partied with friends.

EVELYN. I have a right to a little relief –

VINCENT. Yes you do! I mean, yes I do! I'm stuck in this moldy dump out here on the edge of town, next to a bean field, trying to be responsible, trying to be all that I can to my kids. But what the hell, I'm a young woman –

EVELYN. I'm a human being. Not some breast-feeding machine!!

VINCENT. And sometimes in the middle of the night I get a little crazy thinking about what my life is and what it might have been! So yes, I have a drink or two, or a cigarette so that I can have one moment in the day when I feel free of all that.

EVELYN. That doesn't mean I'm a bad mother.

VINCENT. *(Slowly. He is not sure.)* No, it doesn't.

EVELYN. Okay, then. That's okay, I guess.

(Pause. EVELYN looks at VINCENT.)

You're getting into being me, huh?

VINCENT. *(shakily)* It's my job…to try and see things…

EVELYN. You have kids?

VINCENT. No.

EVELYN. But you have a mother.

VINCENT. *(slowly)* Yes. I have a mother who struggled like you.

EVELYN. Yeah?

VINCENT. And she's proud like you, too.

EVELYN. She have a lot of kids?

VINCENT. Four.

EVELYN. They all smart and professional?

VINCENT. No. But they do okay.

(He coughs for a moment.)

Let's get back to your story.

EVELYN. Your mother didn't get herself in the mess I am in now though, huh?

VINCENT. Oh, she got herself into some pretty bad fixes.

EVELYN. Like what?

VINCENT. *(sliding into a dark place)* Oh…my brother…was difficult. Now you would probably say he was sick.

EVELYN. Is he okay now?

VINCENT. No.

EVELYN. That's too bad.

(pause)

I'm tired.

VINCENT. Me, too.

(resolutely)

But we got to push through this, Evelyn. There are some important points we have to clear up.

EVELYN. What?

VINCENT. Read this. It's a statement from an investigator.

EVELYN. "Footprints were discovered leading up to the spot in the Montrose bean field where – David Laverty's – body was discovered."

VINCENT. Finish reading the statement, Evelyn.

EVELYN. I can't believe this shit –

VINCENT. *(more forcefully)* Read it!

EVELYN. "The footprints in question –"

VINCENT. Finish it, Evelyn. We're gonna' hear it in Court.

EVELYN. Jesus Christ!

(She picks up the paper and continues.)

"The footprints in question…matched the soles of boots found in Evelyn Laverty's apartment. The boots, discovered hidden behind the apartment stove, are size six and a half, the defendant's shoe size and have bits of clinging vegetation consistent with vegetation at the site where the baby's body was found."

(pause)

VINCENT. *(abruptly, piercing the silence)* I don't know how that happened. It's a frame-up. Some one set me up. Maybe that motherfucker, Jack Hoover did this to me. He wanted to sleep with me and I told him off.

EVELYN. That sounds like bullshit!

VINCENT. Someone stole my shoes to take the baby to the bean field and then afterward put them behind the stove.

EVELYN. That's even worse. This is stupid.

(throwing down the papers)

Look, I want to stop this now!

VINCENT. No we can't, Evelyn. We are going to get through this. How can I answer this piece of evidence? What can I say?

EVELYN. Don't say anything.

VINCENT. *(shaking his head)* Come on!!!

EVELYN. Don't!

VINCENT. Yeah, don't say anything. That's what I'll do. I just won't say anything! Yeah, that works. Just don't say anything. That's great! I don't bug my doctor when he blows me off, cause he's the doctor and he should know. I don't hound social services for a crib for my baby, 'cause someone might feel sorry for me! I don't ask my babies' fathers for help cause they might disappoint me! What gives Evelyn? You think that if you keep all that shit inside you that no one's gonna' notice how spun outta' control the situation is. But look at the mess you're in!

EVELYN. Get the hell out of here. I want a new lawyer!

VINCENT. Evelyn –

EVELYN. You're just like the rest of them.

VINCENT. Yeah, that could be. But just because I'm an asshole, one of the hundreds of assholes that you have had to deal with, doesn't change the fact that you have got to speak up for yourself.

EVELYN. Nothing you say is going to matter!

VINCENT. *(Driving. He gets up and pursues her around the room.)* So what! So what! *(firmly)* I am going to try. I am going to look for some words that are going to stand in for something real that has happened to me. I may not get it right, I might offend some people, some people might misunderstand me, twist my words, but fuck it, I am going to speak.

EVELYN. *(Softening. The despair beneath her defensiveness starts to surface.)* What are you gonna' say that'll change anything!

VINCENT. I will tell them about my life with my children.

EVELYN. What difference –

VINCENT. And I will tell them how I struggled –

EVELYN. No one cares.

VINCENT. And I will tell them about the bed.

EVELYN. What?

VINCENT. The bed where I rested with my babies.

EVELYN. *(She sits slowly.)* No. Uh-uh. It's my bed. It's my life –

*(***VINCENT** *stands behind her.)*

VINCENT. I never thought anything bad could come of that bed.

EVELYN. No, I didn't.

VINCENT. It was warm in that bed –

EVELYN. Not ever. No.

VINCENT. After the days I had it was like crawling into paradise.

EVELYN. It was…

VINCENT. When I lifted the covers to join my children, the heat rising from their sleeping bodies…

EVELYN. Warm. So warm.

VINCENT. The smell washed over me…

EVELYN. *(trance-like)* Before I fell asleep that night…

VINCENT. Before I fell asleep that night.

EVELYN. I said a prayer…

VINCENT. I said a prayer.

EVELYN. …that I would become bigger and stronger and smarter. That I would become the mother that my children deserved.

VINCENT. And then?

EVELYN. I fell asleep. Christina was on one side next to the wall and I was on the other. David was between us.

VINCENT. And then?

EVELYN. I don't know. Oh, yeah. I had a dream.

VINCENT. Tell me about it.

EVELYN. We were all together, Christina, David and me... and, this is crazy, we were flying through the air in that bed. And we were over the sea and it was nice but then the sky started getting darker so I was starting to feel a little panicky but then I saw an island. And as we got closer I saw that there were people lined up standing by the shore. And they were dressed in purple robes. Their hands were lifted as though they were trying to catch some rain. Then, as we came closer the people looked up. And I thought, "Look at that! All the people, they're waiting for us. They're waiting! And then...

VINCENT. Yes...

EVELYN. I woke up.

VINCENT. And...

EVELYN. It was gray in the room. A faucet was dripping. And the bed had gone cold. Even the sheets felt stiff. I'm thinking, "Shit, it's another mother-fucking day." And I reach out for David. Thinking that I can maybe stand to get out of bed and start breakfast if I can just hold him for a bit. Even when me and Christina were cold, his body would be hot like a toaster and I wanted to warm myself with him. One minute, God, that's all I'm asking for. One minute with him while he is peaceful. One minute while he is still dreaming of the life he may have. One minute before he wakes up and becomes just this thing who needs me.

(She is shivering.)

But when I reach out for him, he's not there. But there's something underneath me...underneath me... and its hard...like a stone...and the stone is David.

VINCENT. Gone?

EVELYN. *(She gasps as the weight of her awareness hits her.)* Gone. Gone. Oh, no. Oh, God! He's gone.

VINCENT. Evelyn –

EVELYN. My boy gone. I won't live through this. You can't make me live through this –

VINCENT. I can get you out of here, Evelyn. We can get your daughter back. Christina still needs you.

EVELYN. *(Looking for a place to escape her grief, She paces the room.)* Get out! Get away!

VINCENT. Just because your baby –

EVELYN. *(holding her head in her hands)* I'm to blame.

VINCENT. SHHHHH! Evelyn!

(whispering)

This is a defensible case. They can't prove you intended this. Even if you did something that hurt the baby –

EVELYN. He wanted to breathe and I – Oh, my God, where can I go? I got to get out!

VINCENT. There are things you don't know. There are things beyond anyone's control –

EVELYN. Not one thing right –

VINCENT. You have to listen. He was a sick baby, Evelyn.

EVELYN. – my entire fucked-up life –

VINCENT. He had a serious condition –

EVELYN. – no matter how hard I try –

VINCENT. We don't know if he would have survived. Evelyn, we can help you!

EVELYN. *(sobbing)* Not one thing right!

(She grabs at him.)

I'm going under.

VINCENT. I've got you, Evelyn. Hold on.

EVELYN. I can't. I can't live anymore. I can't. I'm going under.

VINCENT. I'm holding on. Holding on to you.

(He contains her in his arms, trying to keep her from blowing apart.)

Scene Two

*(Lights fade on them and raise in **RITA**'s living room where a mournful organ solo plays on the radio as background to an on-air prayer line. A minister is receiving calls of people who are making prayer requests and we hear a few as **VINCENT** walks over to **RITA** and begins to help her with her therapy. He presses down on her foot making resistance that she presses against his hand. As he does this, the calls fade into the background and the organ music plays under the scene.)*

VINCENT. Come on Mom, how about ten more?

RITA. I'm tired!

VINCENT. You can do it. Come on, you could have much greater mobility. One...

(She does some more lifts.)

...two...

RITA. You're tough.

VINCENT. Three, four. I bet Naomi is even tougher.

RITA. You right about that. Okay, that's enough.

*(**RITA** turns off the radio.)*

VINCENT. *(annoyed)* Fine. How are you for groceries?

RITA. I'm out of my cereal, my Entenmann's coffee ring, olive loaf –

VINCENT. Why do you eat that stuff?

RITA. You don't have to buy it. Last time you shopped for me, you bought that low-fat cake. Tasted like cardboard. Naomi will shop –

VINCENT. She's busy with her new job and taking Hector to get his cast changed. Don't bug her. I'll do it after work tomorrow. Are you set for your meds?

RITA. Naomi orders them. You could get me some Ben-Gay from out the cabinet.

VINCENT. Sure.

(He leaves the room for a minute. He shouts from the bathroom.)

VINCENT. Naomi tells me you made it to church yesterday.

RITA. Yes I did.

(VINCENT enters from the bathroom.)

VINCENT. Good for you. Here.

(He hands her the Ben-Gay.)

How was the service?

RITA. Okay.

(She is silent for a minute. There is something she wants to say.)

Everyone at church is talking about the case you on.

VINCENT. *(wryly)* Oh, yeah.

RITA. *(undeterred)* I hear you're gonna get that woman off.

VINCENT. Well, I don't know about that.

RITA. Maybe she'll get a slap on the wrist, that's all!

VINCENT. Hardly, Mom. We may beat the murder charge but even if the jury cuts her a break, she could serve some time and who knows when she will get her daughter back. Now come on, I am not supposed to talk to you about this –

RITA. *(cutting him off)* Maybe she doesn't deserve to get her back.

VINCENT. *(wearily)* Maybe not. I don't know.

RITA. Well, you're doing a job. Sometimes you just have to do a job. That's what I told the Reverend. You don't get to choose the kind of company you keep.

VINCENT. Right…I have to get back to work, now.

(He puts on his coat and gets his briefcase. But he stops and stands still for a moment. When he looks up at his mother, he is clearly ticked off. His jaw is tensing.)

Look, Mama, I know you and all of your other people down at the church have opinions about this woman and what she did but really, Evelyn is all right.

RITA. All right? You got a funny notion of all right.

VINCENT. I just mean she's not all bad.

RITA. What is all right about a woman who kills her baby?

VINCENT. We don't know if that's what happened and even if she did something that contributed to the baby's death, it was an accident.

RITA. That's what she says.

(**VINCENT** *is silent.*)

Do you believe her?

(*pause*)

You can't answer me, can you?

VINCENT. Just because I take a moment to –

RITA. Did she kill that baby by accident?

VINCENT. Yes! Actually, I do believe it was an accident. It was an accident that Evelyn Laverty got pregnant before she knew what she was up against. It was an accident that she didn't have enough money to buy a crib or get more than half-assed medical care. It was an accident that social services forgot that she existed. Oh it was an accident all right. It was a god-awful, pile-up nightmare.

RITA. Listen to you! Cussin' like you didn't know better.

(**VINCENT** *is silent.*)

Did you ever take a moment and think about what she did to her son?

VINCENT. *(trying to stay calm)* Of course I did, Mom.

RITA. With all the opportunities she had. Wish I had – Hmmmph! Left the child in a bean field!

VINCENT. I know that!

RITA. You just say a prayer for that baby.

VINCENT. I'll pray for all of them, for the baby, for Christina, for Evelyn. I don't know that it will do any good. But what the hell, I'll send up a few.

RITA. What's wrong with you?

VINCENT. Nothing.

RITA. You are acting peculiar.

(*Pause.* **VINCENT** *sits down.*)

VINCENT. Mother?

RITA. Yes, Vincent.

VINCENT. *(after a moment)* Why are you so hard?

RITA. I'm not hard. God is hard.

VINCENT. He was hard on you.

RITA. Yes he was. Yes indeed.

VINCENT. How do you reckon with that?

RITA. I had my trials. When I lost your father. When we just about got put out on the street. But he showed me the way. And now look at all I got. I got my daughters, grandchildren. I got you.

VINCENT. What about Ray?

RITA. What about him?

VINCENT. Did God show him the way?

RITA. He shows all of us the way. Just some don't want to take it. That's all there is to that.

VINCENT. Hmmm.

RITA. Don't you give me that "hmmm." I don't like it when you do that "hmmm." I know you gonna' get all lawyerly. Try to persuade me of something, like to take my joint medicine.

VINCENT. Mom, can we talk about Ray?

RITA. I've said all there needs to be said about that boy.

VINCENT. But we need to talk about him. He is missing. It's almost three weeks now.

RITA. He'll turn up as soon as his money runs out.

VINCENT. Not this time. I don't think so. I've been up and down Jericho looking for him and no one seems to know where he is.

RITA. I've washed my hands, son. He's a grown man.

VINCENT. Okay, I understand that but I need to talk about him. I need to talk about him with you. I don't think you remember how close we were. We took baths together. I worshipped Ray, Mom. God! I studied that boy…the same way you study your Bible!

RITA. Look, I did all I could for Ray. Give him money. Got him out of jail more times than I can remember. Pawned my wedding ring. Sometimes I think God sent him to me as a trial –

VINCENT. *(exploding)* Mom, how about we leave God out of this!

RITA. Get out of my house if you're going to talk like that.

VINCENT. *(quietly)* There have been moments during this trial when I would think about you and all that you were facing those years you were bringing us up.

RITA. I am not asking for your pity.

VINCENT. I know. But I want to know you in some other way. To see you as someone other than the woman who raised me. But then you bring God into the picture, and it's like…I don't know…your eyes cloud over and suddenly you, Rita, a woman with a history and with a hard life…you just change into some sort of divine bill of goods and I know that nothing true is going to come out of your mouth.

RITA. Just leave me in peace. Why you try to work my last good nerve? My sugar is gonna start kicking up –

VINCENT. *(exploding)* Why didn't you go out and bring Ray home?

RITA. You want me to go into the city in my condition. I'm an old woman!!

VINCENT. I'm not talking about the present.

RITA. Then what are you talkin' about?

VINCENT. Ray was thirteen years old. You know what happened.

RITA. What do you think happened?

VINCENT. When I was eleven, Ray was gone for a week and when I asked where he was you said he was staying at Aunt Rose's.

RITA. So?

VINCENT. When Ray came back he scared the shit out of me, Mom. His hair was wild. He hadn't bathed or changed his clothes.

RITA. So what?

VINCENT. He had cigarette burn marks on his arms, Mama. He still does. Even an eleven-year old can figure out that he wasn't with Aunt Rose for those seven days.

(**RITA** *looks at* **VINCENT** *hard then looks away.*)

Who was he with?

RITA. I don't know. I don't know. Whoever would take him in, I guess. I couldn't control him.

VINCENT. He was with that pack of blood suckers in the paper mill.

RITA. You don't know that!

VINCENT. You don't want to know!

RITA. That's right! I was doing the best I could! I couldn't go out looking for him. I had the rest of you. Who do you think was there to help me?

(frustrated and angry)

There was only so much of me to spread around, Vincent. Your allergies were so bad I was in the emergency room every other day. Naomi needed help in school. Carrie had to have surgery on her one ear. I had to put everything I had in the ones at home.

VINCENT. Sure and Mister B didn't care for Ray. Hated him in point of fact. You were thinking that maybe Mister B might get off his ass and marry you if Ray wasn't around for a while, right?

RITA. It had nothing to do with Mister B. Ray was always running off.

VINCENT. But this time you didn't go after him.

RITA. I knew he would come home.

VINCENT. Yeah, he came home. And you cleaned him up, put some Vaseline on the burns, combed the garbage out of his hair and sent him up to his room to sort it out all on his own.

RITA. What else was I supposed to do?

VINCENT. When he went back to school after missing that week, his teacher questioned me.

RITA. So?

VINCENT. Ray's teacher wanted to know why he missed school. Wanted to know how he got the burns.

RITA. What did you say?

VINCENT. Don't worry. I lied, Mom. I lied just like you lied to me. I told them that Ray was visiting our dear sickly Aunt Rose in Turnbeck. "He burned himself on the stove when he was heating up her tea." That's what I said. And I guess I was a pretty good liar or she didn't really want to be bothered with another poor, neglected boy. Cause she bought it.

RITA. You did the right thing.

VINCENT. I lied. I was so afraid that if anyone found out…I was so afraid that I would lose you. And I needed you so desperately. I thought I needed you just to breathe. And I didn't care that he needed you, too, and the girls needed you just as badly. I just wanted to breathe.

(pause)

So I lied. You stayed out of trouble, the family stayed together, I didn't miss out on my scholarship to the academy and Ray…well Ray, little fucked-up, 13 year-old boy, the boy you called your tormentor from on high, that defiant, runaway child did not receive one ounce of comfort from anyone.

RITA. So…what do you want from me now?

VINCENT. I just want you to say you are sorry.

RITA. You try and raise four kids –

VINCENT. No one is saying you were a bad person, I just want you to own up to –

RITA. *(unable to relinquish this to her son)* I tried. I did the best I could.

VINCENT. That's not enough.

*(**RITA** is silent.)*

Mother, if something like that happened today, if you let your 13 year-old son run around without supervision for seven days, not reporting him missing or doing something to get him back, do you know what would happen?

RITA. *(unsure)* You think…you think you know everything.

VINCENT. *(slowly but unrelentingly)* I know about the law, Mom. You could lose your kids. If social services got involved and saw Ray's burn marks, well, you might be facing the same crowd that wants to hang Evelyn Laverty out to dry.

(gaining in intensity)

You might be begging all those good folks in this county to please, for God's sake, cut you some slack!

RITA. Are you trying to kill me? You just want me to just lay down and die, don't you?

VINCENT. *(backing down somewhat)* No. No. I'm trying to understand…that's all. Trying to cut my way clear to something like truth.

RITA. *(darkly)* You will never know the truth of my life. Children never know.

VINCENT. Maybe not.

(He pauses.)

You are my mother. You brought me into this world. I guess you love me as best you can. But we don't know each other.

RITA. I guess not.

VINCENT. Maybe someday, I'll be able to see you as just another person staying alive in this world and maybe someday you'll be able to do that for me, too.

*(**VINCENT** looks at her a last time and shakes his head. He leaves the house silently. **RITA** stands in the middle of the room looking after him. She is still for a moment. Then she reaches up and slowly takes off her glasses and drops them. She swipes her cane at the remaining trophies and picture frames and knocks the entire array down. When the shelf is bare she stands there breathing heavily.)*

Scene Three

(Lights come down on her and come up on **VINCENT** *is in a courtroom delivering his closing argument in Evelyn's case continuing on from the speech we heard at the top of the play.* **EVELYN** *sits on another part of the stage. She is in another time and space, answering questions posed by an off-stage prosecutor.)*

VINCENT. *(pause)* Consider now, ladies and gentleman of the jury, consider now…another woman. She is sister to her ideal. But unlike her sister, this woman is not eternal. Unlike her sister, she is solid with muscle and weighty with time. To see her in the flesh is to be reminded that lives are short and our bodies will betray us. So it is hard. But consider this woman, for she is demanding your attention at this moment.

(pause)

Consider the woman who birthed you.

(pause)

A woman who went through the pain of hard labor…

EVELYN. We moved into an efficiency apartment on the edge of town. It was a converted from a garage.

VINCENT. A woman who cried out…

EVELYN. They didn't have a crib for me at the time.

VINCENT. Who has limits on her store of time and good humor…

EVELYN. No, I didn't complain to no one. I should have complained.

VINCENT. A good person, capable of astonishing acts of resourcefulness, who can also be selfish, lazy, improvident…

EVELYN. Yes, I drank at night. Sometimes. Not every night.

VINCENT. A person who serves but also one who craves…

EVELYN. I thought some day I would get a GED.

VINCENT. …solitude, some new clothes, time to daydream.

EVELYN. I needed beer…and cigarettes…to get through the day.

VINCENT. She is willing to sacrifice but at times, at night, after a long, difficult day, she might ask herself if the sacrifices that she makes to bring up her children add up to a good life.

EVELYN. I tried to give my children a good life.

VINCENT. She is not the mother of your dreams.

EVELYN. I didn't want Christina to see him like that.

VINCENT. But she is your mother.

EVELYN. I took him to the bean field and lay down with him.

VINCENT. Evelyn Laverty is not the mother of your dreams. But she is not a murderer. There are facts to deliberate in this case. Will you deliberate the facts?

EVELYN. We had a party. A little girl from Christina's kindergarten class came over and we played some games and blew bubbles. One of them landed on the baby and I swear, he reached up his little hand to grab it. The girls were pretending to be mothers, putting David on a blanket with their dolls and changing his diaper. Everyone was fed and warm and happy. And I thought to myself, "It's going to be all right. I can do this. I'm a good mother."

(Lights come down.)

Scene Four

*(**VINCENT** sits at the defense table in the courtroom staring after his client being lead away. His briefcase leaks paper. After a moment, he picks up the disheveled paper and jams them into his briefcase. Then he puts his head in his hands. **MAIA** enters and touches his shoulder.)*

VINCENT. *(starting)* Leave me alone, Maia!

MAIA. You got the lesser charge!

VINCENT. I made her soft. It will go worse for her now.

MAIA. She needed to be soft.

VINCENT. She was already soft. Too soft.

MAIA. I can try to get her some consideration in her placement. A few years with time off –

VINCENT. Good, you take on that placement thing, will you?

MAIA. I'll fix what I can for her. But Vincent –

VINCENT. Yeah, see what you can organize. Uh huh. And while you are at it, why don't you see that what's-her-name, the little girl, Christina, remembers she had a mother, could you? Because, you see, not to be rude or nothing but I am done with all of it –

MAIA. Vincent. Stop all this now. We'll work out an appeal later –

VINCENT. Life goes on with a vengeance, huh? I've heard about boundaries. Never been too good with that!

MAIA. Vincent…I know about Ray.

VINCENT. Oh…that.

MAIA. Your mother called. She's trying to reach you. She wants you to be with her when she goes to identify the body.

VINCENT. She has her daughters. Her church.

MAIA. You don't know how she has suffered through all this.

VINCENT. No, I don't. She won't give me that satisfaction.

MAIA. Vincent, "consider the woman who birthed you!" You demanded that from your jury.

VINCENT. I think they call that "courtroom oratory."

*(He pushes his briefcase toward **MAIA**. He looks at her for a moment and takes off. **MAIA** calls off.)*

MAIA. Vincent…Counselor!

(She starts after him and then stops, taking stock. After a moment, she takes in a breath, gathers up Vincent's briefcase and papers and then walks out of the courtroom, her shoulders squared to face her work.)

Scene Five

(Lights come up on the bean field at twilight. **VINCENT** *walks in. He comes to a spot that has the remnants of a police investigation. Some orange tape remains. A make shift shrine has been set up by some people in the town. There is a cross, a sign that says, "We love you, Baby David," a pile of stuffed toys, etc.* **VINCENT** *picks up a flower.)*

VINCENT. Oh, boy. Oh my goodness. Baby David. Twenty-two days on this earth. For twenty-two days you lived tucked between your mother's rib and the soft side of her good arm. And the rhythm of her breath and the pulse of her blood became the code for everything… all you were meant to do or be. And then things fell apart. Like they do, sometimes.

*(***RAY*** appears in the shadows of the train trestle in silhouette.)*

(turning slowly) You're here.

RAY. You didn't think you'd get away from me just like that?

*(***VINCENT*** turns around and is transformed to his younger self.)*

VINCENT. *(starts to move away, looking back at* **RAY***)* Just stay away from me! Back off, Ray!

RAY. *(moving toward* **VINCENT***, grabbing his collar)* Where the hell you think you are going?

VINCENT. *(Breaking free. Elbowing him in the ribs.)* I said leave me the fuck alone!

RAY. *(reacting to the blow)* You little shit! I would kick your ass into kingdom come but I don't want Miss Rita to get a case of nervous aggravation!

(cuffs him on the ear.)

Come on, she's waiting.

VINCENT. She don't have to worry. I'm leaving now. Let me by.

(They do a little dodge and feint and this continues as the next few lines of dialogue.)

RAY. You dropping off the face of the planet, bad-ass?

VINCENT. I'm dropping off the face of this town, that's for sure. Get the hell off me –

RAY. What! You think you are gonna' slip into the fuck-up slot! Uh, uh! No sir, that slot is mine for the time being. I ain't giving that up yet. Uh, uh. That slot will retire with King Ray's name on it before I let you slip into that shit.

(They stop parrying. **VINCENT** *is panting.)*

(gesturing to a old crate in the field)

Sit down. You're getting yourself all excited.

*(***VINCENT*** sits down.* **RAY** *stands off while* **VINCENT** *calms down.)*

VINCENT. I can't live with her anymore. I'm not a person to her! I'm just the kid that gives her bragging rights at the church.

RAY. The woman's got to have something to brag about, don't she?

VINCENT. You never go to school. Don't do shit in the house. You just show up and eat and Mama lets you run wild, do all you want. The girls are in votech. That shit is easy. They get out at two, hang out at Frankie's Hamburgers most the days. Why am I the one has to go to the private school where everyone treats me like some charity case!

RAY. Cause you can!

VINCENT. You could, too. You're just as smart as me.

RAY. No, I ain't. I can't stay out of trouble to save my life. Now that is crazy stupid!

VINCENT. *(standing up)* I'm going.

RAY. Oh yeah? Pressure gettin' to you?

VINCENT. No. Shut up. I just want to make some decisions for myself.

RAY. Oh. Okay. What you gonna' do?

VINCENT. I don't know. Find a job. Hop a train.

RAY. And what about your scholarship to the academy? What about all the people who stood behind you?

VINCENT. I didn't ask for anyone to do anything.

RAY. You didn't ask your mother to bring you into this world. But she did.

VINCENT. Why are you always defending her? What did she do for you?

RAY. She does what she can do, given the nature of her limitations. Miss Rita's all right, man.

VINCENT. She's a self-righteous, Bible-thumping hypocrite.

RAY. Yeah?

VINCENT. And I'm sorry. I think she could have done better by you. Better by all of us!

RAY. Oh God!

(trying another strategy)

So how come you never say any of this to her?

VINCENT. She wouldn't listen.

RAY. You just a big old phony, ain't you. And now you just gonna' run away from it all, that it?

VINCENT. Yeah.

RAY. Mmmmmm. You just never could get over that I was her favorite child.

VINCENT. Oh, come on!

RAY. I ain't saying I was the likeliest child, but brother, look me in the eyes now... I am her favorite.

VINCENT. You! Get out of here!

RAY. Me, okay.

(grabs him by the collar)

My mother loves all her children – all of them, you hear – but I was the first-born.

VINCENT. All right. I'll give you that.

RAY. And I am the favorite.

VINCENT. *(Softly. A discovery. Even relief.)* Okay, okay. You're the favorite.

RAY. *(moves away from* **VINCENT***)* Now listen, Vincent. I ain't always gonna' be here for you.

VINCENT. What do you mean? Cut that shit out.

RAY. I am just – not to be all grim about it or nothing, man, but like I said, I ain't the likeliest child…everyone knows that.

VINCENT. Shut up, man! You just saying that in case you start getting fucked up again.

RAY. Maybe. But of all of us. Not just in the family, but all of us living out our lives in this stretch…you are the one.

VINCENT. Don't put that shit on me, man. I can't take it.

RAY. I didn't put it on you. And Miss Rita didn't neither.

VINCENT. Then who?

RAY. Let's leave that one for the philosophers. Come on, brother, dinner's on the table. And you know Miss Rita ain't one for letting her table go cold.

(He playfully swipes at **VINCENT** *and it escalates into a little wrestling. They are cursing and laughing at the same time. Finally* **VINCENT** *has* **RAY** *in a bear hug. They stand in a kind of awkward embrace, panting.)*

VINCENT. Do I have to go back?

RAY. Oh, yeah.

(They wrestle some more. Then they pause, panting.)

VINCENT. But, no, come, on Ray, no. I don't –

RAY. You got some shit to work out, brother. Come on. Let's go!

*(***RAY** *tries to break free and* **VINCENT** *holds on releasing his pent-up worry, concern, love, burying his face in Ray's coat.)*

Hey, now. Easy does it, brother. I'm here. You're okay. You're just fine.

(He comforts him for a moment and then, softly)

RAY. *(cont.)* Let go now. You'll be okay.

*(Slowly he pries **VINCENT** away. The lighting changes. **RAY** begins moving slowly back into the shadows as **VINCENT** comes into the present. As he does **VINCENT** begins to address his lines to the sky rather than to the retreating **RAY**.)*

VINCENT. Will I?

RAY. You'll be more than okay.

VINCENT. All right, then.

RAY. You will be your mother's consolation.

VINCENT. What! I have to go there?

RAY. Oh yeah. Time to slip the skin of self-righteousness!

VINCENT. Oh that!

RAY. Busted!

VINCENT. Damn you!

RAY. New generation, same ol' shit.

VINCENT. *(taking a breath)* Okay. Hold on a minute!

RAY. Give it up, now!

VINCENT. All right. All right.

(finally)

She will have my arm in consolation.

RAY. What about the heart?

VINCENT. *(He struggles for a moment. Then)* I'll get to work on that!

RAY. *(jubilant)* "And they will call him wonderful!"

VINCENT. Oh, no. Now he's quoting the Bible!

RAY. I am my mother's son, no doubt.

VINCENT. No doubt about that.

RAY. You got to get moving, Brother. You have some personality reassessment to do. You got to try one more time.

VINCENT. I spend a lot of time doing personality reassessments, don't I?

RAY. You sure do. But it's time well spent. Nothing's wasted.

VINCENT. Oh, no!

RAY. Everything is everything.

VINCENT. Yes it is!

(RAY disappears into the shadows. It starts to rain. VINCENT walks back over to the shrine. He kneels down.)

Nothing wasted. Nothing wasted at all.

(RAY disappears. VINCENT looks up at the sky. Rain starts to fall. He looks up and lifts his hands like he is going to catch some rain.)

End of Play

OTHER TITLES AVAILABLE FROM SAMUEL FRENCH

A VIEW FROM 151ST STREET

Bob Glaudini

5m, 3f / Crime Thriller / Unit Set

A View From 151st Street incorporates elements of spoken word poetry, takes a look at life and death on the titular street in uptown Manhattan. An undercover cop is undergoing rehabilitation after a shot to the head. As he re-learns words and recovers his memories, a coke-dealer turned wannabe rapper spins into a downward spiral. Cops, rappers, dealers, teachers, hustlers, husbands and wives dwell in the rhythms of rap, raw humor, aphasic staccato and live jazz.

SAMUELFRENCH.COM

CPSIA information can be obtained
at www.ICGtesting.com
Printed in the USA
LVHW082056291018
595205LV00032B/900/P

9 780573 699122